Province of Fire

Province of Fire

Geraldine Connolly

IRIS PRESS

Cover watercolor by Christine Neill
from *Canna and Rodo* diptych (1997)
Courtesy of Gomez Gallery, Baltimore, MD

FIRST EDITION

ISBN 0-916078-46-9
LIBRARY OF CONGRESS CATALOG CARD NUMBER: 98-88641

IRIS PRESS
1345 Oak Ridge Turnpike
Suite 328
Oak Ridge, TN 37830

www.irisbooks.com

—for my grandmother, Adella Blazikowski

Acknowledgments

Cafe Solo: "Chance Meeting"

Chelsea: "Where the Wave Begins," "Sorrow's Dress"

Connecticut Review: "Movie Queens"

Cream City Review: "Dream of the Past"

Defined Providence: "Harbor Song"

Elm: "Astronomer"

Excursus: "Number Seven Mine," appeared as "Past the Corner, Opening Gate"

Faultline: "God in His Loneliness Above McKeesport"

Flyway: "Why I Was Sent to Boarding School"

The Georgia Review: "Procession of All Souls"

The Gettysburg Review: "Grotto"

The Hampden-Sydney Poetry Review: "Hair of a Teenage Goddess" appeared as "My Daughter's Hair"

Hayden's Ferry Review: "The Future"

Maryland Poetry Review: "White Silk, Hope Chest," "In the Province of Fire"

Monocacy Valley Review: "Stanislaus"

Oxford Magazine: "Savannah Live Oak"

Plum Review: "Place of Vines"

Poetry: "New World"

Poetry Ireland Review: "Mornings of Silence"

Publication of the Society for Literature and Science: "Siberia"

Poetry Northwest: "An Afternoon in the World," "Doll Suitcase"

South Florida Poetry Review: "Black Glass Along the Railroad Tracks"

West Branch: "Blue Bridge," "Unexplained Territories"

"Islands" appeared in *What's Become of Eden: Poems of Family at Century's End* (Slapering Hol Press, Tarrytown, N.Y., 1994).

"One Death" appeared in *For She is the Tree of Life*, ed. Valerie Kack-Brice (Conari Press, Berkeley, California, 1995).

"Blue Bridge" was reprinted in *Anthology of Magazine Verse* and *Yearbook of American Poetry 1995/96* (Monitor Publishing, Palm Springs, California, 1996).

"Past the Corner, Opening Gate" and "The Way She Could Disappear"appeared in *Getting By: Narratives of Working Lives* (Bottom Dog Press, Huron, Ohio, 1996).

"The 1937 Dodge" appeared in *XY Files: Poems on the Male Experience* (Sherman-Asher Publishing Co. Santa Fe, New Mexico, 1997).

"Daughter at Thirteen" appeared in *The Practice of Peace* (Sherman-Asher Publishing Co., Santa Fe, New Mexico, 1998).

The author gratefully thanks The National Endowment for the Arts and The Cafritz Foundation for their support.

Contents

I

II

III

IV

I

WHY I WAS SENT TO BOARDING SCHOOL

to lengthen my hem lines and straighten
my morals

because I was difficult

because my parents were tired

to lock me in chastity's cupboard

to Latinize me, teach me manners,
give me a good solid dose of fear

to place over my face the mask
of stoic cheerfulness

to take away my swagger
tame my wild hair and rebellious tongue

because that's where the doctors
sent their daughters

because the nuns would know
what to do with a girl like me

because they would do their best
to pour me into the mold

with china limbs and lace collars
and because my parents had
their fingers crossed

that I would come out nice
like a floral centerpiece you could
put right into the center
of your dinner party, gleaming

as heads of cut flowers
bobbed there, grateful, arranged
blinking and nodding with grace
saying *yes, yes, turn me*
and they would turn me
from what I was
into what they wanted

not the wolf girl
not soaring beast with smoking hair

but a tame Hereford
amiable, smooth child they could love
with no thoughts that were devil-born
a flat good prize of a girl

and there where I looked
into a morning mirror
I would encounter myself
calm, bovine, accepting

beloved of Mother Superior
cherished of God the Father.

PROCESSION OF ALL SOULS

Gnarled and blessed
be the hour of autumn when
spotted pears sink
into wet sod and blessed be
the songs of virgins rising
into hunchbacked trees.

November dawn.
Down damp stone stairs
we followed the priest
past leaf-choked wells
and jagged trees,
past a red rage of dogwood
ringing a black lake.

Dies Irae, he intoned,
Dies Illae, day of wrath.
We followed his swinging
censer, trail of smoke:
schoolgirls in gray, novices
in white veils, nuns in ragged black
tapping tortoise canes.

What joy to bear the fear,
smell orbs of incense
perfuming the rot of leaves,
to cross the stubbled field
as crows rushed and whirled,

pecking at windfall seeds.
We arrived, rainsoaked, awed,
to watch young nun-brides
kneel, and spread their thin bodies
across green doors of graves.

MORNINGS OF SILENCE

At boarding school with the nuns, the rule of silence
prevailed, stiff finger raised to lips, pressed
hard to keep them shut. Like St. Theresa,
and the Virgin Martyrs, we were admonished

to stay silent, composed, to go inward
during the early hour of rising and dressing,
attending a mass that Father Ryan, with aged limbs
and speech impediment, labored to celebrate.

We sat through it in grim silence, as if under water,
half-asleep at dawn, whole mornings of silence, our
white chapel veils sliding off uncombed hair,
not imagining the mysteries, not meditating,

but thinking of the wayward girls we were told
were herded once into this very chapel,
brought here from the prison farm nearby,
guarded by men who carried rifles

and sat in the row behind them in the oak
carved pews with red leather cushions on each
kneeler. Sometimes one of us would keel over
and faint, thudding into the aisle, or have a nosebleed

to break the monotony of silence during the stone hours
of Lent, labyrinth of prayer and response,
vigils and complicated devotions.
In every one of us lived a prison girl—

a convict who strutted back from the Communion
rail, sullen and leering, skirt hiked up
as far on the thigh as she could manage,
flaunting her boyfriend's ring on a gold chain

hung from her neck, swaying between
breasts that he had touched
near the red lipstick tube and black mascara wand
with gold cover jammed into a blouse pocket.

We filed up in silence, knelt in silence,
white adolescent torsos like marble
statues stacked up in hallways and church pews,
brooding land mines waiting to explode.

Catholics

We had incense and black-frocked priests,
smudges of ash smeared across our foreheads,
wafers of God in our mouths, while meek
as Pascal lambs, feet encased in Sunday shoes,
hands in gloves, missals in purses, we filed up
church aisles to take whatever they handed out—fear
in Latin syllables and irate sermons, rosary beads
clicking against pews, stacks of holy cards
with rosy saints emblazoned among shining rays
of fractured light. It meant thorns and crosses,
scapulars of felt with Joseph's face in a soft plastic casing
hung on strings around our necks, removed
with care each night to bedposts. It meant bishops
in tall hats with long frightening croziers,
slapping children to teach them to be soldiers.
It meant plates of fish and meatless Fridays,
macaroni and tuna casserole, abstinence.

It meant penance, contrition, genuflecting and confessing.
It meant kneeling and rising in fear of light-struck monstrances,
ice-cold golden chalices filled with pieces of God's body,
chilling bells that splintered our hearts. Being a Catholic
meant *way of life*, meant boarding the great ship
of Holy Mother Church and staying put when it went aground.
We could go to any nation in the world and still finger our beads
and chant the Latin Mass, bending our heads beneath rules
that would not bend, rules stiff as pieces of wood the priest
beat us with. And we could take it. We were the faithful.
One, Holy, Roman, and Apostolic, we were clusters
of sheepish men in ill-fitting suits and crewcuts,
we were haggard wives and scores of dogged
children streaming up the church aisles to take
Communion or drop folded dollar bills pinched

from wages into offering baskets that floated Sundays
down the pews. And each week we would kneel
on wine-colored velvet, before the grillwork screen
and face the priest's black bulk of shadow
and he would take our whispered sins into his body
in the dark carved oak of the confessional booth
and swallow them, for our own good, as we had been swallowed.

SEWING CLASS

Steep cobblestone hill and a rain-slicked sidewalk,
teacher waiting in the school I climbed toward
with her thick brogans and long stick that struck
like a cobra when seams were too short or crooked.

How I ran, my breath gone sharp into my throat,
leaves of slick damp stuck to my shoes. I ran as the children
ran when the wolf huffed and blew down their hut.
All the cars stopping at lights moved on, leaving me adrift,

nose running, coat flapping, watch ticking past the hour
when class began. And the great buses I had no quarter for
rose up, took the hill and spewed exhaust. One glove gone,
hair in shambles, I ran as each wave of black rain

lapped against my shoe tops. And the slippery hill,
cobbled stone, slowed me. My heart thumped, a caught falcon—
Late! No yellow school in sight, only bare sycamores
rearing up, giant matrons pointing fingers, asking where I'd been.

THE SUMMER I WAS SIXTEEN

The turquoise pool rose up to meet us,
its slide a silver afterthought down which
we plunged, screaming, into a mirage of bubbles.
We did not exist beyond the gaze of a boy.

Shaking water off our limbs, we lifted
up from ladder rungs across the fern-cool
lip of rim. Afternoon. Oiled and sated,
we sunbathed, rose and paraded the concrete,

danced to the low beat of "Duke of Earl".
Past cherry colas, hot-dogs, Dreamsicles,
we came to the counter where bees staggered
into root beer cups and drowned. We gobbled

cotton candy torches, sweet as furtive kisses,
shared on benches beneath summer shadows.
Cherry. Elm. Sycamore. We spread our chenille
blankets across grass, pressed radios to our ears,

mouthing the old words, then loosened
thin bikini straps and rubbed baby oil with iodine
across sunburned shoulders, tossing a glance
through the chain link at an improbable world.

Movie Queens

We cut them, languorous, compelling,
from empty backdrops, propped them,
one atop a horse in a riding suit,
one at lunch on a cruise ship
skimming a bay in California.

Clusters of dolls leaned
against cement blocks,
a garden of pale faces
above shimmering lilts of cloth
and color, fox fur stoles,
ornaments of pearl and sequin.

We believed in what we could
become. We'd never have to earn
a thing, only stand in a rage of beauty
as clothes fell from the sky
in sumptuous heaps

and we vanished
into evening gowns, cashmere wraps,
leaving black thoughts,
sweating bodies, dim hours
for a cold, dry paradise.

GROTTO

Small pond
statue of the virgin

drying fountain
cracked rosary

mottled stones
tracks in the mud.

Bliss blooms
somewhere

a secret
flower behind

a private door.
Beneath heavy drapes

limbs move
in the dark, stripped

free, light
of the body aglow,

a rush of pleasure
like a fish

swum up from
a sunken orchard.

An Afternoon in the World

I remember how the nuns
spit it out, hissing—
the word *secular*,
as Rosie and I slithered
past school down the hill,
to the shopping mall
and gorged ourselves on candy,
hot chocolates, forbidden movies
among soft-lit, carpeted boutiques.

Escaping evening rosary
again, we descended
to North Hills Shopping Center
to rise on long, shining escalators
into a paradise of costume jewelry,
evening wear and perfume atomizers.
After days of the words *discipline*
and *spiritual*, after the dry
prayers at breakfast, at lunch,
choir practice, piano practice,

forced study hall, devotions
in chapel at Angelus, Vespers,
we hurried through squadrons of clerks
into mountains of stacked dry goods,
draping paisley shawls and strings of pearls
over our dull gray uniforms,
dabbing Crepe de Chine,
Canoe, Jungle Gardenia
onto our wrists, slipping

into sling-backed leather pumps
with stiletto heels, pulling
long silky nylons and garters up
our secretly shaved legs.
Where are you now, Rosie,
and where are those fuzzy sweaters,
electroplated rings, that orange
yarn we bought and spooled
around our boyfriends' class rings
before we hung them
from our necks, that bright pink
polish we slathered over them
in a sticky heap, and the
lipstick with silver flecks that
tasted of rainwater? Where
are those tortoise shell compacts of blush,
the mascara wands? As if a wand
and a sweater could turn us
into models and not those
gray-blazered schoolgirls
in oxford shoes and high socks

running back up the road
hugging paper sacks of merchandise,
running hard, having stayed
too long, rushing so as not to
miss supper, and holding
that taste of the secular
beneath our tongues
like those bright-colored
candy rings we favored,
lemon, watermelon, lime
and cherry, those lifesavers.

II

BLUE BRIDGE

Praise the good–tempered summer
and the red cardinal
that jumps
like a hot coal off the track.
Praise the heavy leaves,
heroines of green, frosted
with silver. Praise the litter
of torn paper, mulch
and sticks, the spiny holly,
its scarlet land mines.

Praise the black snake that whips
and shudders its way across my path
and the lane where grandmother
and grandfather walked, arms
around each other's waists
next to such a river, below
a blue bridge about to be
crossed by a train.

In the last gasp
of August, they erase the time
it might be now, whispering
into the darkness that passed,
blue plumes of smoke and cicada,
eager and doomed.

The Way She Could Disappear

Adella stepped up
from steerage and leaned
against a stair rail,
long braids wound into a knot.
The gray skirt hung,
dusty with old world dirt,
plain and foreign
among the flour sacks.
She liked the way she could disappear,
one face among a sea
of faces, roulette-like,
whirligigged: onion domes, slashed
crosses, children wheeling
dizzily on bicycles, a woman sweeping
the street with her broom.

Beneath high buildings, she passed
windows made of thin glass,
ringing trolley cars, a blind man
with one leg, selling gladioli.
Coke ovens blasted their smoke
but she flew by, going to the edge
of where she would like to be,
passing through into greenness

to the county with that name—
Somerset. She wanted a farm.
She wanted a safe place
where she could be at peace,
even though
she would pay the price,
never part of the old life now,
nor part of this.

MENDON

Beets sweetened in the straw basket
and rains poured
from the downturned lake of sky.

Each wet morning her hands kneaded
dough and pulled, sliced the rye loaf
on the pine cutting board,
pinched white geraniums to send

ghost blossoms up the windowpane.
Her reflection spun like a lightning wheel.
Then she rolled rice and meat
into pockets of cabbage, counted them,
smothered them in sauce.

When she sat down to sew,
bad ankle stiffening,
she placed the patch of silk
next to a square of tweed,
then plucked one silver button
from the jar of dark ones,
resolved to make something new.

Gleaming thread drifted
like a thought
through the needle's eye.
She knotted it
and pierced the cloth.

STANISLAUS

Patience, he thought
trudging the long muddy road
in the morning fog.
The trees wore his wife's hair.
Lunch bucket. Headlamp.
He went down into the earth,
into the black damp,
weight of air thickening,
strap-on tools and belt and pick
pulling him down—
chokedamp, stinkdamp,
afterdamp—into the basket
with strangers, dropping
into that other world.
He went after the black veins
with pick ax, chisel.
Tear off the chunk of coal.
Move on.
Shoulder to shoulder
miners packed the tunnel
so tight they
could barely breathe.
Broken rocks and splinters
scattered. From far away
he thought he heard
the hooves of mules
thud and clank
from the world.
That tiny light from his
partner's lantern
burned through the shaft
and led him on
as if it were the North Star
rising off his sooty forehead.

ANGEL OF DEATH

Shawl on the head,
beer in the tavern,

Adella's children
persevered.

A bible of descent
held their names

written in coal dust
marked in a village hand.

Though the angel of death
stood behind the bells

and blew a tin horn
in the shadow

of hung-up beef
among branches of knives,

handed-down shoes,
rivers of hourly wages,

when the time came
and he took one,

it was her husband.
Among jugs of whiskey,

eggs in vinegar,
he left only

a keepsake lock of hair.

NUMBER SEVEN MINE

—Stanislaus Skavinski   *(1883-1926)*

After that carload of coal swerved
his spine was crushed,
and his sons forced to work in the glass factory.
They carried tin lunch pails down
past the corner to the opening gate.

Nightfall, they returned
to read to their young sisters
from the book of stories
with a dog that looked up from
the engraving at them,
saucer eyes aglow.

The dish ran away,
said the youngest
my mother,
ran away with father.
His sons breathed in smoke
as they worked,
deafened by roaring gears.

Grinding down, doubled over,
they scrolled braided wheat sheaves
onto the dazzling glass.
Vase after vase, they stamped and sealed,
sent down the line, one to hold

flowers from the cutting garden.
Each piece held the glaze of their
sweat, grit of purpose, each rim encircled
their father's absent gleam.

and the rims of her shoes
digging forward into the dust
along the path to school.
If she leaned into
the steel rails she could
still feel the heat
of the train that had passed
and if she leaned back,
the pull of the house,
her mother alone
in the sweet dark of her room,
asleep on the white sheets
she rarely left.

Curves of the track,
bodies that enter a life
and leave. When her father died,
they walked up the stone stairs
to the church toward the white hair
of the priest. She'd never
forgive the men in black suits
from the coal company. Some even
shouldered the coffin's dead weight,
then stood, heads bowed in mock
respect. Even now, this morning,
a whistle from the first shift
shudders through her
like a blow.

ODE TO COAL

You are the hard heart
through which
each message passes,

the black stone of thought
brought down from the mountain
to burn for God.

You are the flint of anger
and the black veins
hidden, stealthy.

You are the hard bed
that immigrants
sleep upon.

WHITE SILK, HOPE CHEST

Against the window, rain falls in a veil
from the broken gutter. My mother fingers
the heft of a fabric, its gravity.

A river of cloth feeds the black machine,
undulating reams poured into silky dream,
farm with an orchard, apple trees, cool silo.

Organza dresses spill forth, satin underthings
trimmed in ribbon for her daughters' hope chests.
Outside her window, rain makes history vanish.

She tears off the ripped seam of disaster,
crash in the coal tunnel, her father killed, mother
bedridden, shakes off a knot of memory to lift

her daughters' lives from the selvage of the past.
Their life is the one she is creating now,
well-cut, supple.

THE PLANT

In the dark, in his work clothes, my father set off
for the iron gates of the Westinghouse plant.
There, before a fire, apron and goggles donned,
he'd pour molten plastic into a mold,

then let the great cooled rings descend on pulleys,
crack them open with his muscular arms,
release them into shapes of sun and wheel.
At noon whistle he took his tin lunch pail

beneath the tall oak's long shade,
and ate ham on rye from a wax paper sack,
chased it with boiled eggs and lemonade.
He looked skyward, thought of Canada,

each white cloud like his wooden boat afloat
in Shawanaga Bay two weeks each summer
in the Thousand Islands. He'd steer his craft,
great Evinrude motor strapped to its stern,

across shoals, through channels and inlets.
The plant, he called it, the place where he worked.
No dragonflies or blue heron appeared,
no sunsets as in the minnow-filled shallows

where his children swam frog-legged
and rose chilly and wet among the dragonflies.
Here he was a fish whose hour had spiraled
away as the whistle blew and gears turned,

while time clocks ticked and the screech
announcing the next shift jarred
his bones. Then he streamed back
with the others, swarming into the net.

PROSPERITY

As we got home from school, mother was leaving,
our mother in her white waitress uniform,
hair pulled back tight, bobby-pinned and hair-netted,
    black apron tied on.

Soft spongy shoes with thick soles and crisscrossed laces,
shoes brushed with chalky polish framed her ankles.
She'd pull on her orange nylons thick with sparkle,
    tuck the striped notepad

into a pocket along with a miniature pencil,
dab a spot of perfume behind her left earlobe,
and shrug on a plain cloth coat, snapping her purse shut.
    She'd grab her keys,

jangle their silver, left hand slamming the door
as she headed through the breezeway to her car.
We'd make tuna casserole, watch *Love of Life*
    or play solitaire.

After midnight, we'd hear her Plymouth roll in.
The heaven she chased was called prosperity—
blonde dining room suite, curtains for our kitchen.
    She bought winter coats

for us, velvet collars, muffs, berets to match.
She brought home paper bags full of leftovers,
veal Marsala, chocolate cheesecake, and mousse.
    They were sumptuous

and though I wanted to lick sweet, rich icing
from sponge cake, and to snap the crisp shells off
Gulf shrimp, dip them in cocktail sauce, I wouldn't.
    I ate none of it.

New World

In the overheated apartment
of my mother's uncle
in Chicago on North Ash Street,
mushrooms, white sausage
and sauerkraut simmered in a pot.
The little nut-filled horns
lay next to the apricot ones
on a doily on a tray
and a silver frame encircled
the past in the shape
of my great uncle, a Polish soldier
from World War I, holding
a tall rifle. Foreign words
floated around my ears.

Around the cross-stitched cloth
of the dining table,
the grownups lingered
in oak chairs. They ate
to erase the memory
of thin crops, soldiers
routing them from haystacks.

But I needed to remember—
Latin declensions for exams,
notes of Haydn for piano solos,
steps to my dance
in an embroidered headdress,
its long ribbons fluttering
against my shoulders
above the puffed sleeves
of my peasant blouse.

Apprentice to new ways,
slave to the old,
my heels skipped across
the blonde, varnished wood
of the gymnasium in America.
Someone had made this journey for me
and I must continue the story.

BAPTISM

I could see they were perplexed
since I wasn't an infant
but a girl of nearly nine,
tall by the font,
embarrassed at my size,
standing with my sister who was four,
both of us having lived until now
in a state of original sin.

They couldn't hold us like infants,
smooth and innocent, so they let
the water flow over our hands
in pure rivulets of mercy,
I suppose. Too old,
awkward, I didn't answer
what was true. My mother's
expulsion from the sacraments
confused me. Because of her sin—
divorce, she hadn't been
truly married in the Church's eye,
until her first husband died.

Gripping steel rosary beads,
suddenly legitimate,
I stood there beyond the age
I should have been, holding
a white stole emblazoned
in yellow thread
with the Constantin cross,
a quiet lamb beneath it,
meek and pious at this witnessing.

In the year of Our Lord, nineteen
hundred and fifty-five, God hauled up
two more souls, my sister and me,
baffled, unwilling,
holding our candles aloft
into the vaulted mouth.

THE 1937 DODGE

Left by my father's Uncle Wesley
to his nephews,
the shining car sat
undriven in a closed garage
for twenty-five years
while the three brothers
fought over his estate.

It rested among rusting
oil cans, jars of nails,
behind the bolted double door.
Fine machine, I would hear
the uncles say,
mint condition, a beauty,
as though speaking
of some virgin of youth
longed for and never possessed.

It perched on its throne
of heavy blocks,
and never moved,
while Esther, Eleanor, Dorothy and Bess
married, grandmother died,
the house crumbled,
vines snaked up,

looters smashed windows, lamps,
hacked up the furniture,
while the brothers could not
make their fortunes or settle
their dispute. And the great
Dodge shone, colossal
in its tomb.

God in His Loneliness above McKeesport

The nuns flew back and forth from church
to convent to school, black wings
of conviction and purpose. They loved
God in all his loneliness and the children
of the immigrants, fresh, white-faced,
who lined the pews with hopeful bouquets.
Shadows jammed the aisles, sins
overflowed the confessionals.

On the river, the whistle blew
at daybreak, noon and night shift.
Debris floated, vials, shiny wrappers,
bottle caps, past the mill fire
that lit the night sky and exploded
in a thousand sparks. Reverent
with abandon, we held out our arms
to catch them.

III

THE MOVIES

Holding Dixie cups and candy straws
against summer breezes, we strolled

along narrow avenues
to the blinking marquee

of "The Lamp" whose ticket window
glowed. We gave our quarters

to the hand that reached out,
then flipped back a red ticket—

entrance! We had aspirations
to the loneliness of paradise

where horses and corrals sprang up,
pirate ships, Egyptian faces,

long kisses igniting the screen,
shoot outs, the orange of apocalypse.

We sat through charlatans and lepers,
slapstick idiots, a shining man

who ascended in his robe
into sunset-streaked clouds.

Then we stumbled back,
music still roaring in our heads,

to drugged sidewalks
under monotonous awnings

with the price of corn and potatoes
where reality swam up

like a full Friday dinner plate
whose gray fish we could never finish.

CHILDREN OF THE TRAIN

—for my brother

When a trembling
started up,
shook a curve of evergreens,
we were up and running.

Two lit eyes
out of the tunnel first,
a small blunt head
and metal streak
of cars rocketed the track.

Whistle rush
through smoke blast.
We were pure terror
of speed, heat and hot metal

as the rolling stock
of flickering
windows and sleepers,
coal cars, freight cars,
overwhelmed us,
goods heaped high,

the weight of industry
passing,
until that tiny man
in the very last car

stepped out, hand raised,
to greet us,
two thin children waving
from a field of wayside flowers.

ONE DEATH

When my grandmother was dying
in her soft bed in the corner
of my aunt's farmhouse kitchen,
we all sat with her, even the children,

staring at her white, shut face,
masked in a rapture of its own
while all the noisy racket of death
filled the air, lungs letting go,

blood about to rise in a purple wash,
the pot of bones knocking
in a fury to stay behind.
Or perhaps the soul was rattling

its grip, a last hold on life,
giving the body one final slap,
she shuddered and trembled so, then
shook it all off and turned away.

I knew when the spirit left, her body
cold and floury, still. We gave her
bed rail one last shove, helping
give her over to whatever pulled at her

from that other world. She no longer waited
as women wait but held forth one arm,
buoyant as that white branch the angel brought
both to warn and to comfort.

At the Funeral Parlor

We sat with grandmother, weeping, wiping our noses,
telling stories, surrounded by a waterfall of forced flowers,
baby's breath, roses that lay strangled with ribbons.
One by one, we rose up and went to the kneeler

with its crushed velvet cushion. I bent there,
fingers pressed into a spire as I examined the shell
of her, closed eyelids, purple mouth, beads of rosary
entwined in crimson loops among stiff fingers.

Your daughters look like movie stars, whispered
an old woman to her shut face. I tried to imagine her sweeping
a floor streaked with coal dust or frying trout in a skillet
with egg noodles, buttered cabbage. I conjured the house

they lived in amidst bluebells and wild mustard
next to a spring house whose cool water flowed
into her daughters' hands. I wished I had seen her
young, handing a ladle of spring water to her husband,

one wisp of hair fallen from her temple, him lifting
his hand gently to her forehead, to smooth it back.

SORROW'S DRESS

I let the seams out,
put them back in.

How I love the rip
of silk across skin,

the cold rush
of renunciation.

How I love
the broken threads

of loneliness, more
than sorrow itself.

I tug at anger,
pull its seams

until the dress of joy
becomes misery,

its dark skirt
of pleasure tight,

which suits me

as no happiness
could.

Cinnamon and flutes,
silent roses,
    wisteria.
I could have said I loved her.
I could have lifted the gravestone
and spoken in the forgotten tongue,
the husks opening as the world would
in May, a rush of heat, of summer.

    I could have
cried out when she was dying,
lifted a hand against the angel's sword,
or hidden her soul in the work basket.
I could have said, *October. I will meet you
on the twelfth day, under the plum tree
behind the crumbling spring house.* I could
have lost the ribbon of forgetfulness
behind the attic stairwell, or spread
the cinders of lime across the garden,
with its stubble of grief, its shards
of coal, in that country field behind the wet sheets
billowing from a clothesline like clouds of milk,
cherry branches among scrubbing boards,
our little world of ox-eyed daisies,
village church bells, broken fences.

    I am lingering
in that tunnel we hoped to dig to China,
broken doll arms among the heavy
spoonful of earth we began with,
her rumpled bed in the corner
of the summer kitchen,
the ice of absence
next to an open window.

PEONIES

With long stems, top-heavy, erect on juicy stalks
along the gray ocean of horizon,
you stood in a row behind the dim garage
where we dumped eggshells, ash, coffee grounds.

Novas seen with the naked eye, primadonnas
among marigolds and bean vines, your lava
spilled, dazzling, into giant explosions—
galaxies of hot pink comets, like our passions,

stifled into green coats, Sunday manners.
We longed to burst into life's drama, vivid as you,
drinking the dizzy air, but too young, we ironed
while black ants climbed into your folds and drowned.

DOLL SUITCASE

Little empire of Barbie,
rectangular, snug, safe,
with a white plastic handle
and tiny lock, before lovers
or husbands opened it
into rapturous disorder.

This was longing, girlish,
doe-like, for forget-me-nots
and trelliswork, a satin gown
in ice blue, bell-skirted
with shoes dyed to match,
a first kiss wreathed
in significance at twilight.

Our desire, quiet and cool,
hung there on plastic hangers
like the tiny clothes, puffed,
frilled, perpetually adrift.
The red plunge neckline dress
floated. Its white tulle skirt
flared from a bodice dotted
with red hearts that interrupted
a chaste white sea of skirt.

Hearts lived there, red
as the boy's flushed face,
red as the scratchy bricks
behind my shoulders as he
pushed me against a porch wall,
staining satin, crushing his boutonniere
of pale chrysanthemums.

The hoarse sobs, the fumbling
words we gave away,
took back, and gave.

DREAM OF THE PAST

Slow creak of oil and ropes.
Faint bulbs in dim halls.

Doors shut like eyelids.
And then stairs open. I spiral
dizzily, my heavy valise
weighing down one arm.

Smashed eyeglasses,
spindly wreaths
and peeling numbers.

I've come back at the wrong hour.
The key is here somewhere
in the slant light, in its secret
hiding place, under horsehair,
on a long, pale string.

Night Shift

Mill town, half light.
Half of nothing is still
nothing. Soot falls
on your skin. Broken
lights stutter
and gasp
above dirty windows
of corner saloons.

Nuns cross the street after Vespers
to Holy Trinity Convent.
They climb the stairs
of these high hills
where shouts rise from the river
of faces like bad luck.

Men enter the mill as a rope
of dark ants winding
into a hill of sand.

SIBERIA

In railway tunnels
next to burning escalators

are passages into
departed cities.

We enter the shaking tunnel,
dark heart of the carriage.

Brush strokes of light appear
in the icy windows.

Moving through the soft dusk
like streamers, we pass

over bridges, cross piles
of lumber, abandoned cars,

complex pipe tubing
of refineries. The locomotive

pulls us with its fierce body,
through fencing,

strange tongues of night
porters, morning's despairs,

to begin and begin. Hard forests,
the crooked hours, vanishing

towns. Decades arrive
where I look

into the lit windows
and watch my birth,

bloody and glorious in one,
my wedding night in another,

all the aunts and uncles
dying or tending the unborn

gathered at a table.
I see the one aunt

who was left behind
in the old country. I see

the room where I will die.
Passengers shake like so many leaves

through the Siberia of evening,
departing, heading away.

I write this to you
against the February snowdrift,

the long days and sharp branches,
to make apologies and introductions.

I send you my body in this white
envelope, my soul in its contortions.

I cut this ice into the pieces
of a life. I cut it holding

the scissors like a hot knife,
making rags of eggshell threads,

pointed and sharp. I look
for the straight hem and cut it.

I look for the strong secret
threads, the knot

that will not open,
the faces that we remember,

insufficient, singular,
night's border, advancing.

IN THE PROVINCE OF FIRE

(James Hampton, sculptor, 1909-1964)
The Throne of the Third Heaven

What Christ would sit on this throne
of radiant, alarming tinfoil,
turrets and wings, butterflies of cardboard?
What god would speak from this pulpit
intoning the words of Moses and the prophets
announcing them from crooked tablets
covered in scripts of unknown meaning?
Who would decipher these urgent messages?

A janitor of the discarded,
a prophet of the lonely—
who stayed in his garage through the night
and lettered, on a makeshift platform
cardboard tablets bearing
the New Testament, the Old Testament,
the history of the Millenium.
He drew and painted, nailed crowns
of purple art paper to the throne's back,
one for the east wind, one for the west,
God's wind blowing through all that is forlorn

even to this cold and simple rented garage
on N Street where the seat of the Great One
waits, empty. The janitor's monument
spread, its great shining balls of crumpled
aluminum covering castoff tables,
exploding into crowns and snowflakes.

While revelations expanded in his head,
he, most faithful of servants, God's carpenter,
shaped wings and raised swords

into a glory of jagged lightning bolts,
apocalypse of wood and paper.

The poor will stand in his first circle,
luminous, when God takes his seat
on the tinfoil throne among the rays
of foil-covered light bulbs.
He will lift a paper crown
from the dusty floor to place
on the head of one who has labored
in dim light with glue and straight pins
and has not been afraid.

IV

QUILTING

February. Hanging
icicles, music
of passage as they break.
Toward the light
that frames her we look
at sorrow, at the little coffins
of pattern that engage her,
sheltered by stitching.

Her needle, her weapon,
would like to break
into blossoms of smoke,
of leaf, transparent grace,
the true wildness
within her.

LIGHTNING

Fish bones rise
in the black trees.

For a moment, distance
does not exist.

The world cracks open
into the past.

I had imagined
her death

like this,
a white rage,

a bridge suspended
over narrows,

then the bridge
falling.

MOTHER, A YOUNG WIFE LEARNS TO SEW

Those were the days
she slipped a silver needle
neat as a minnow
through a piece of cloth.

It went swimming
up and out
of the river of fabric
guided by her hand.

Was that glance up
at the open window
a happy gaze, or a cry
to be outside, running, free

through carpets of garnet
vines or azalea blaze,
not pushing the steel point
of an instrument through linen,

not putting hooks and loops
and buttonholes in order,
staying to the task, keeping on,
baste and stitch, as the world burned
and glittered and she held on
to purpose and industry.

Wildwood-By-The-Sea

One good dress a year is all you need,
she said, adrift in her white cotton
Chinese sheath, three crimson letters
slashed across its sleeveless bodice. In white
high-heeled sandals, she is about to go dancing
with my father on the deck of a seaside hotel.
He wears a plaid bow tie and a grin;
her dark hair is loosened from its chignon.
Mother's mouth shines, bright as a dogwood berry
and the strange Chinese words climb
her right breast like painted daggers.
Good luck, or disaster?

I have found the dress in an upstairs closet,
its cloth so light and smooth now, the red rope of belt
vivid, each end knotted as her stubborn will,
each foreign word wild as her temper,
though on the night I saw her wear it she was soft
as polished cotton and the evening a language
she danced through, speaking in tongues.
I touch one embroidered word lightly
as I unfold and it turns into the arrow she shot
through his heart, the one that kept him
pinned to her while the rest of us remained outside,
watching their unbroken circle of gaze and tilt
as they twirled across a patio above the raging sea.

THE FUTURE

My son's hair darkens a shade each day
although when I look to the window
the only view is straw barbs, wild, golden,
that stiffen into autumn. Straw of his hair,
thorn apple. The kernel of him was
once planted inside me, away from harm.
Male flower, goat's tongue, the hard
berry of him erupted in kicking.

I love the violence in him
as I love the sweetness.
At birth, his body emerged
from the hive in a storm.
If only I could recall
a way into the future,
the way his legs lengthen
and stalk, the way his hair
grows and darkens. Pushing
on the sill, I raise the window. I let go
a little more of him each day,
my blood flowing into the world.

AFTER HER BIRTH

My breasts had hardened into marble geysers
and the surgery scar rippled across my lower abdomen
the first morning they brought my daughter. I was eager

but thrashing limbs caught me by surprise,
the piercing cries of the baby, her contorted face
shaking. My contractions throbbed as

she burrowed, a fish mouth pulling at dry air.
When she slipped I almost dropped her,
milk dripped down my skin, the sheets stained

with it. Unable to find the breast, she struggled
against me. Not the portrait I had imagined,
mother nursing newborn daughter in sun-flooded

room. In the Giotto, the mother is composed,
her head coifed in linen, the child tiny and pale
as if her skin were light rays, or porcelain.

A Jamaican nurse intruded, took the raging baby
and leaning over, grabbed my breast, clamped
with sure force the mouth against the nipple,

pressed hard, holding the head firmly to it until
she latched on, a monkey riding the slope of my flesh,
pulling. *Do it like this, mama, get serious.*

Don't be foolin' with her. I felt my body's weight
diminish, emptying into her. One totemic figure,
we swayed while the blood of afterbirth spilled

from my womb, the milk pumped through
into her sweet mouth and my hand held her firm
while she sucked, took her fill and finished.

DAUGHTER AT THIRTEEN

In capitals scrawled across her notebook,
she letters the names of boys she loves.
The names change. She crosses
one out darkly, adds a new one,
sketches a heart stabbed with arrow.
Her hips sway, her earrings
that are small fish dangle and leap.
Her words pick up speed,
rush out in cascades. She dances to hiphop
and rap, makes her hair punk.
She shakes down her frizzed locks,
runs her fingers through them
when meeting a gaze, and turns,
clean and sharp as a silver blade,
to dive into her room.

She whispers on the phone, then
emerges, shouting at us. Posters of crows,
clenched fists, young men with torn
t-shirts and sullen gazes grow
from her fleur-de-lis wallpaper.
All we get is resistance from this girl
who is about to bristle open.
She sends out charges,
the sparks of her new being, prickly
and burred. When we draw near her,
a dazzle of pure light shines.
We draw back, let it continue.

ISLANDS

In that frightening home movie,
I am thirteen. It is summer,
my hair long, tangled.
My mother butts against me, playfully
at first, then harder. She is pulling me
into the mother and daughter film,
meant to record us, happy.
It catches instead my furious face,
arms tightened around my own shoulders,
then her pulling my arm too hard,
pulling me down the rocky hill
of our vacation into the camera lens
where green pines swing fragrantly.

I have almost escaped but my mother
grabs my long hair in her fist,
pulling me to my knees. A fighting fish
she's hooked, I'm refusing
to be her prize, ready to strike her.
My arm's raised. Why hasn't my father
stopped this film? He could have stepped
from behind the camera and put his hand
between us. Can't he see a wall
must be put up, a barrier
between our furious wishes? Two islands
that have grown together, we can't
separate. We each face head on
that part of ourselves we hate,
mirrored in the other.

REGRETS

Out of their secret places
in autumn, from under

dark logs and smooth gravestones
they come, black snakes,
stripped, floating free

in the golden September sunlight
which drifts as they try
to hold onto it.

They lay their bodies
across our warm paths,
branches of misspent hours,

limbs from low gullies.
Past school children and old men
they wind, making no sound,

sliding the earth in silence,
riding a world that seems dull
and hazy, half-spent,

beautiful errors
that rise up as we gasp.

While the Others Worked

I hid behind a book,
shirking, not helping
with the cutting and slicing,
boiling and sugaring.
In my room in the dormer,
I lay behind the shut door
on my bed reading a novel.

My hope chest with its treasures
of pillowcase and table linen
rested below the window sill.
This is where mother had placed
her hopes for my future, where
a house with a long green lawn waited,
ready to receive silver teaspoons,
bone china and crystal salt cellars.

The chest itself looked like a house,
spacious and solid. One by one
the goods to fill it were cut and stitched
according to some formula
that had nothing to do
with my pens and notebooks.

Beyond ideas, her dreams
were finished and laid
in this tomb of great possibility,
wrapped in soft tissue
among cedar blocks.

MY FATHER AT HIS CARPENTRY

The buzz of his saw is deafening
among odors of linseed and turpentine.
He cuts a slab of pine down, scattering

curls of shavings with the universal cutter.
Teach me to smooth my passion's rough edge
and not to bludgeon, but finesse and ease.

Show me what to learn about a fitted corner,
how to ease things with a smoothing plane,
after you balance the level across joint and seam,

how to labor for the sheer pleasure of labor,
as shapes swim up, forgotten, known,
becoming one with wood's knotted dream.

BEEHIVE

An angry bee circles the zinnias.
This morning, memory is bitter as I comb my hair.

I remember her comb tugging, catching
my tangled knots, her hand pushing

against my child skull as if it were stone,
making the hair taut as wire, to straighten

the curls into thick plaits. Then she clipped the ends
and banded them, the lack of tenderness unexpected,

a little ritual of mother and daughter ruined
by tears and tension, harsh as the fact of her absent

father, torn away from her at age three.
I remember that hair of hers, never twisted free,

but swept up, lacquered, wound
thick and luxurious into a tall mound—

formal, the way beauty was for women then,
unapproachable, something that must be earned

through suffering, or denial, hair high in relief,
stiffened into a style they called "beehive."

Hair of a Teenage Goddess

When she shakes it,
it takes on a life of its own,
grassland, wing flutter,
cascade of sea ferns.

She has been waiting
all her life for this hair
and sits for hours,
brushing it, braiding it,
twisting it into coils
that she lets fall
into sprays of streaming curls.

When she comes from a distance
her hair floats before her.
The mother is frightened
by its power, afraid
the girl could burn, or drown
in its splendor. Ropes
that burn a yellow path
between them sway
above the girl's pale shoulders.

Thirty Years Later I See

after Frank O'Hara

I was a woodpecker
banging against iron authority.

I was a wildfire in the play yard
who loved cat's eyes, hard marbles,
the glassy stares of flying bass
caught with my own rod.

If anyone was looking for me
they could find me in my fort
of birch bark and dogwood leaves
planning sorties.

Now the woodpecker's flown away.
And the tree. I've become the tree
limbs sprouted from my waist
as the leaves thin and fall.

Children peck at me.
My parents lash themselves to boughs.
The bonfires of the enemies
burn through my crevices.

ASTRONOMER

When I had trouble waking,
Galileo would step forth
in the foggy dawn
with his galaxy of order.

His hands hung down
large as my father's,
so large they looked
like small animals
as they fed doves,
brushed away spider webs.

I gave him a twig
I'd found on the snow,
one brown fern stuck
to it, like the uncombed hair
of a young girl late
for school again.

A mother raven shook
her black wings in the rain.
Storms rose up, volcanoes
erupting into clocks
that sped too fast.

He gave me a mirror.
In each pane of its glass,
a pair of daughters
held hands, two white poppies
trembling in a dark field
while a father
calmed the waters.

Savannah Live Oak

This oak, like the sturdy
trunk of his body,
ascends—strong legs,
taut calf muscles,
long straight fingers.
I love my husband's
lips and teeth, his sharp
wit, gentle tongue.
Leaves crackle and spin.

The yard spreads open,
green–gold in sunlight,
shining bamboo,
low azaleas everywhere,
blazes of purple
and pink. I stop.
Oak leaves swirl up
and my hands move down,
pick up a brown one
the color of his hair.

Hot sun burns.
As I sweep, each
strand of broom straw
pierces each
crisp leaf.

Harbor Song

I love breakfasts
in far off cities,

men in dark sweaters
among china plates

heaped with sausages
and fried potatoes,

ships outside
in the port, named

Phoenix, Osiris,
your cool shoulders

beneath the striped shirt,
mirrors dividing

into flares of salvia.
Raspberry jam

smeared across a biscuit.
Shining cutlery, open books,

ribbons of milk,
all the resurrections

we need
about to happen

this day
and afternoon and night.

Whirring Journey

Two hummingbirds soared across the book's page.
We stood stunned, at the brightly colored maze—

two beaks caught, four wings whirring in bliss.
Swift against the twining, your hand touched the page

then brushed mine. *Feed a winged one honey, feed it loss.*
I remember a kiss after you stroked the ivory page;

Near a dusty museum shop on a side street,
we lingered, touching. Page after page

of splendid mornings turned to luxurious noon.
There's comfort in returning to this distant stage,

my name, now, an autumn berry suspended
from your lips, fire on a glittering page.

In the supermarket after lunch,
my lost grandfather emerges,
the man who died
before my birth,
heavy-footed, Slavic,
wearing the high cheekbones
of the provinces, a hat
with earflaps, a long scarf.
He tugs on my sleeve
and asks "Shoo-gar?"
his eyebrows lifting
like jagged pine boughs.

I lead him
past mayonnaise and pickles,
pyramids of apples,
to the blue sacks of sugar
stacked like Polish matrons.
He thanks me shyly.
I can smell wine
on his breath from lunch,
drunk from a green,
long-necked bottle.

I can taste bread
and sausage, feel the pinched
shoulder from that night
he slept on a rock in a field
next to the strip mine.
A bright railroad ticket
to Pennsylvania shone
in his right fist. He had

just stepped forth from
the twelve-day voyage,
having left behind Franz Josef,
a sickly mother,
and his firstborn daughter.
Aloft now
on a migrating wind,
he lights up the aisles.

Invisible raindrops slip into the grass.
I notice them turning the yard into deep mossy caves
and recall my mother as a girl.
She sits in the past while I imagine the child she was,
in a dress with sprigs of hyacinth sprayed
across the cloth. She was sassy with dark coils of curls.
I like to think of her up in front of the class
for the math contest, giving the right answer.
I watch pansies flutter in the wind along the latticework,
think of how she became pregnant at eighteen,

became a mother too soon, no longer carrying
cornflowers she herself picked, with wild violets
slender and vibrant shining in her hands,
but cooking, laundering, tending children,
planting and canning, scrubbing and sewing.
Mourning doves rise like handkerchiefs waving
to the future. Their duties are to their heartbeats.
Her life was work and family, a frantic whir of gathering,
saving. My duty is recording, choosing to paint
the afternoon into a mural of words.

But I cannot give the girl
her childhood back, nor can I invent
a magnificent ending. I can only sit here
and think and make streaks across a page,
pen strokes that are light and sure. To paint
the morning is good. It fills the hours with pleasure
as more drops fall, changing the world
in slow degree, changing.

STREAM

Behind the back porch,
behind the chicken yard, beyond the first corn field
and low stand of pines, its ghostly deer;
beyond the creek and the shifting tribes of cattle,
beyond dawn and morning and muddy noon, beyond
gravestones and salamanders, a tail feather of water trickled.
Its darting tongue of silver turned into a stream and flowed
over black chipped stones, scratchy pools of lichen,
musky nut-filled loam of earth, ran among caterpillars
and pine needles, dropped holly berries and
pleasantly flowed, forgetting torn coats and lost buttons,
slights and mistakes, forgetting suffering, not remembering,
knowing only flow and whorl of rush, invisible grace
of evaporation, knowing attention to the leaves, bits of straw
and lace-winged mayflies. Water moves from where it's been
to where it's going with complete avidity across dry fields,
across pebbles of oblivion. Cool water in grandmother's basin,
warm water in the claw foot tub, boiled water
around the salted calf's tongue. Water in the creek
where the cats were tied into a sack and drowned. Well water,
spring water, flood water, bright zigzags of ice across
the windowpanes when we woke, thirsty, our breasts hurting
with growth. Bright green water we smacked into,
making fountains of spray at the end of the water slide.
The rainbow waters of Niagara Falls, striped
like a Halloween wig, rose, and the waters of Baptism poured
over our unwrinkled foreheads. Water filled the bay
where minnows hid in the reeds and water held
our vine-covered canoe, shallow and dark,
filled with longing, Water gushed from me,
hot and blood-streaked with the body
of a son and a daughter.

PEARS

They remind me
the dried fruits she sent—
tart apples, cherries, pears
of the way
her life was shrunk,
turned into some diminished thing.

They loaded the family
furniture onto a truck
when her father died.
She stuffed three silver dollars
into a sack and held it
on her lap. I bite the hard
memory in two
but there's no going back.

She's frozen there
at four. Those new shoes
she left in a closet in the box
waited for her return. Her brother
lifted her onto the stack
of baggage and she held
onto her coins.

In the city where she arrived
girls skipped across cracks
in a sidewalk. She held onto
her sack of coins, looked
straight ahead remembering
the way her life had been—
a golden pear on its own plate.

Where the Wave Begins

Under my pillow where the wave begins
a child is about
to be swept under.
She wandered here,
dazed, and can barely manage
the sea's edge.
Picked up, tossed high
along the wave crest,
she rides, about to be
flung into undertow
in her white cloth diaper.

I am reaching for her
but the wave is so high
her hand eludes my grasp.
Just before waking,
at the very height of terror,
I see she is my mother.

I reach out and try to grip her,
pull her to warm sand,
blanket, thermos of milk
and wake
not knowing whether
I have pulled her back
or let her go,
her small handprint
pressed like a burn
into my hand.

About the Author

Born in Greensburg, Pennsylvania, Geraldine Connolly grew up in Westmoreland County and was educated at the University of Pittsburgh. She worked on the staff of the Folger Shakespeare Library from 1971–1975 and attended graduate school at the University of Maryland. She has received two fellowships in poetry from the National Endowment for the Arts, one in 1987 and one in 1995. In 1988, she received a Works-in-Progress grant from the Maryland Arts Council and in 1990, a Maryland Arts Council Fellowship. She was the Margaret Bridgman Fellow at the Breadloaf Writers Conference and has held residencies at Yaddo, the Virginia Center for Creative Arts and the Chautauqua Institute.

Her chapbook, *A Red Room*, was published by Heatherstone Press in 1988 and a full-length collection, *Food for the Winter*, by Purdue University Press in 1990. She recently co-edited *The Open Door*: an anthology of work from *Poet Lore*. Her work has appeared widely in literary magazines, including *Antioch Review, Chelsea, The Gettysburg Review, Georgia Review, Shenandoah, Poetry*, and *Poetry Northwest*. She was awarded the Carolyn Kizer prize from Poetry Northwest magazine in 1989 and won the National Ekphrastic Poetry Competition in 1998. Her work has been recorded and broadcast on WPFW Radio's "The Poet and the Poem." She teaches poetry at the Writers Center in Bethesda, Maryland and at Johns Hopkins' Washington D.C. Graduate Writing Program.

Colophon

This book was set in Monotype Bembo which was based on typefaces cut by Francesco Griffo for the printing of *De Aetna* by Aldus Manutius in Venice in 1495. *De Aetna* was written by Pietro Bembo about his trip to Mount Etna. Griffo's design is considered one of the earliest of the Garalde Oldstyle typefaces which were the predominant text types in Europe for 200 years from the early sixteenth through the seventeenth centuries. The Oldstyle Roman typefaces are still widely used in contemporary texts because of their classic beauty and high readability. Stanley Morison supervised the design of Bembo for the Monotype Corporation in 1929. The italic of this typeface is modeled on the handwriting of the Renaissance scribe Giovanni Tagliente.

The paper in this book meets the guidelines for permanence and durability of the Committee on Production Guidelines for Book Longevity of the Council on Library Resources. This book was manufactured in the United States of America by Thomson-Shore, Inc.